THE BABY BEEBEE BIRD

Diane Redfield Massie • PICTURES BY Steven Kellogg

NEW TO THE ZOO

For Daniel and Leanna Hardy
—D.R.M.

To Peter with love
—S.K.

The Baby Beebee Bird   Text copyright © 1963 by Diane Redfield Massie   Illustrations copyright
© 2000 by Steven Kellogg   Printed in the U.S.A.   All rights reserved.   www.harperchildrens.com
Library of Congress Cataloging-in-Publication Data   Massie, Diane Redfield.   The baby beebee
bird / by Diane Redfield Massie ; pictures by Steven Kellogg.   p.   cm.   Summary: The zoo
animals find a way to keep the baby beebee bird awake during the day so that they can get some sleep
at night.   ISBN 0-06-028083-2. — ISBN 0-06-028084-0 (lib. bdg.)   [1. Zoo animals—Fiction.
2. Sleep—Fiction.]   I. Kellogg, Steven, ill.   II. Title.   PZ7.M42385Bag   2000   99-33421
[E]—dc21   CIP   AC   Typography by Michele N. Tupper   1 2 3 4 5 6 7 8 9 10   ❖
Newly Illustrated Edition

HarperCollins*Publishers*

R

EEEEEEEEEEEEK EEK EEEEK

AKKKITY AK

AK

AK

EEEEEK

arga arga

ga

The animals at the zoo had roared
and growled and hissed and meowed
all day long. They were very tired.

hisssssssss hisssssssss

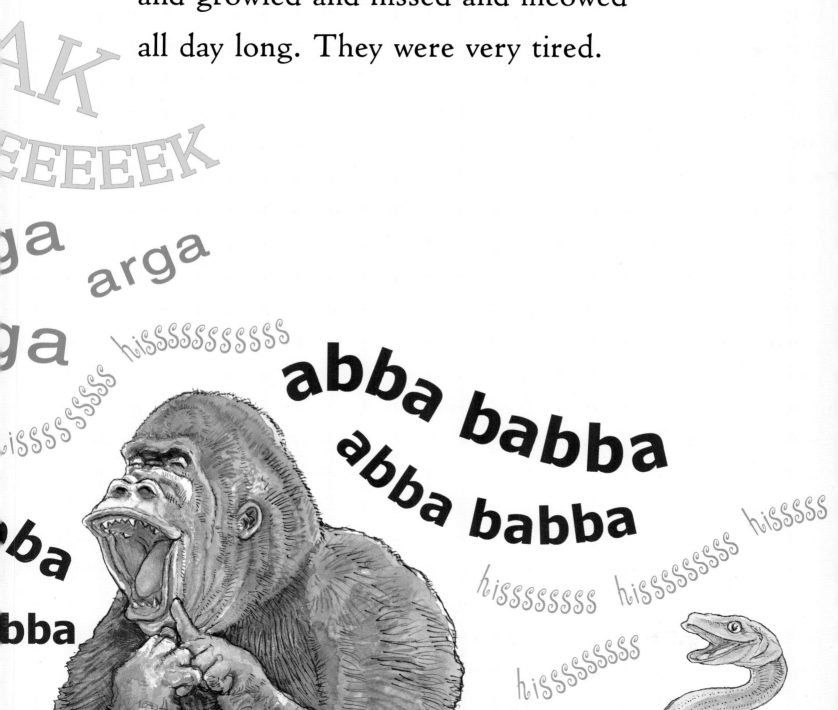

abba babba

abba babba

ba

bba

hisssssss hissssssss hisssss

hissssssss

"It's eight o'clock," yawned the elephant,
and he settled down in his big hay bed.
"I've eaten 562 peanuts today," he said.

But no one heard him. They were all asleep.

The zoo was very still . . . until . . .

"What,"
said the elephant,
"is THAT?"

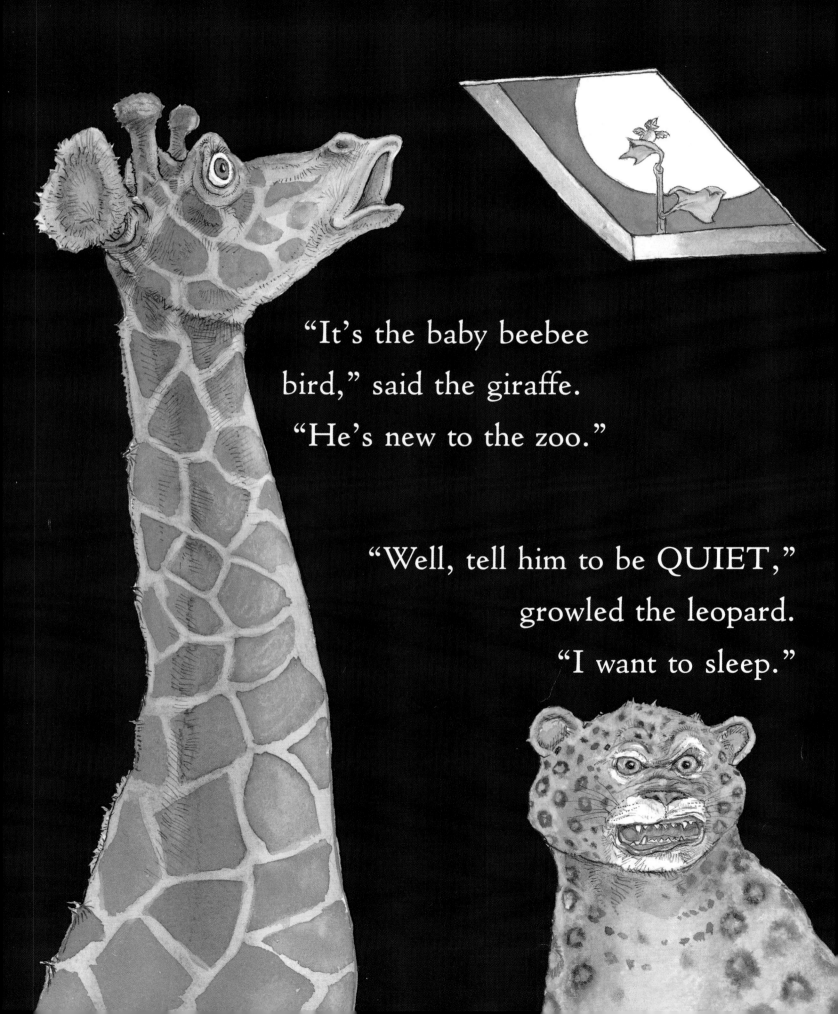

"It's the baby beebee
bird," said the giraffe.
"He's new to the zoo."

"Well, tell him to be QUIET,"
growled the leopard.
"I want to sleep."

"Be quiet, please," said the giraffe politely.

"But I can't,"
said the beebee bird.
"I'm wide awake."

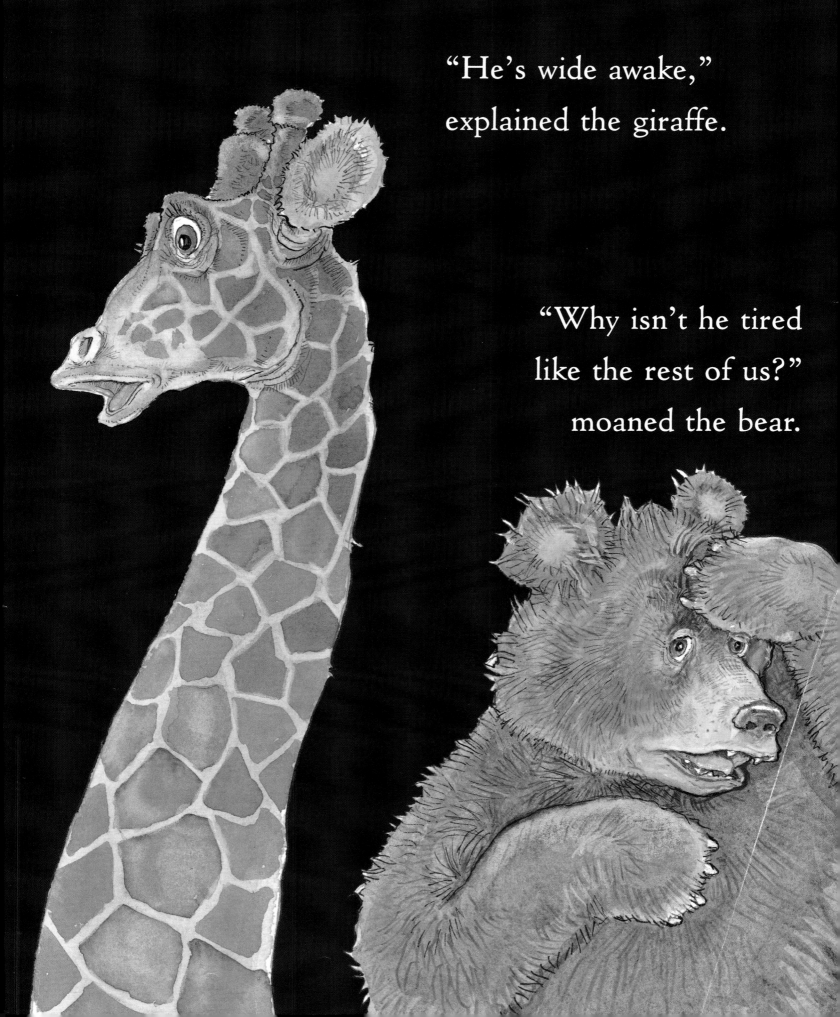

beebeebobbibobbi beebeebobbibobbi

"He's wide awake,"
explained the giraffe.

"Why isn't he tired
like the rest of us?"
moaned the bear.

beebeebobbibobbi beebeebobbibobbi

"Oh dear," said the elephant, "and I am so sleepy."

"QUIET!" shouted all the animals.

beebeebobbibobbi beebeebobbibobbi

"WE CAN'T SLEEP!!!"

beebeebobbibobbi beebeebobbibobbi

all

night

long.

The sun rose in the morning on a very tired zoo.
"What can be the matter?" cried the keeper.
"The elephant is still lying down."

"The lion's paws are over his eyes."

"The eagle isn't screeching."

"Oh, dear me, the animals must be sick!" he wailed.

And he hurried away.

"Beebeebobbibobbi," said the baby beebee bird cheerfully, and he settled down for his morning nap.

beebee
bobbibobbi
beebeezz
zzzzzzzzzzzzzz

The lion
whispered
to the bear.
"I have a plan,"
he said.

The bear
nodded,
and
whispered
the plan
to the others.

The beebee bird
was at last asleep.

"BEEBEEBOBBI," roared the lion.

"BEEBEEBOBBI," trumpeted the elephant.

"BEEBEEBOBBI," bellowed the bears.

"BEEBEEBOBBIBOBBI!
BEEBEEBOBBIBOBBI!"

sang all the animals together.

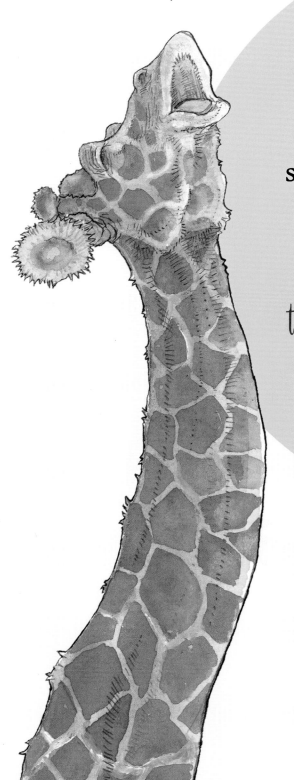

"QUIET!"

said the

beebee bird.

"Can't you see
that I'm sleeping?
It's time for my nap!"

"BEE BEE BOBBI," yelled the hippos.

"BEEBEE BOBBI," shrieked the seals.

"BEE BEE BOBBI," thundered the moose and the water buffalo.

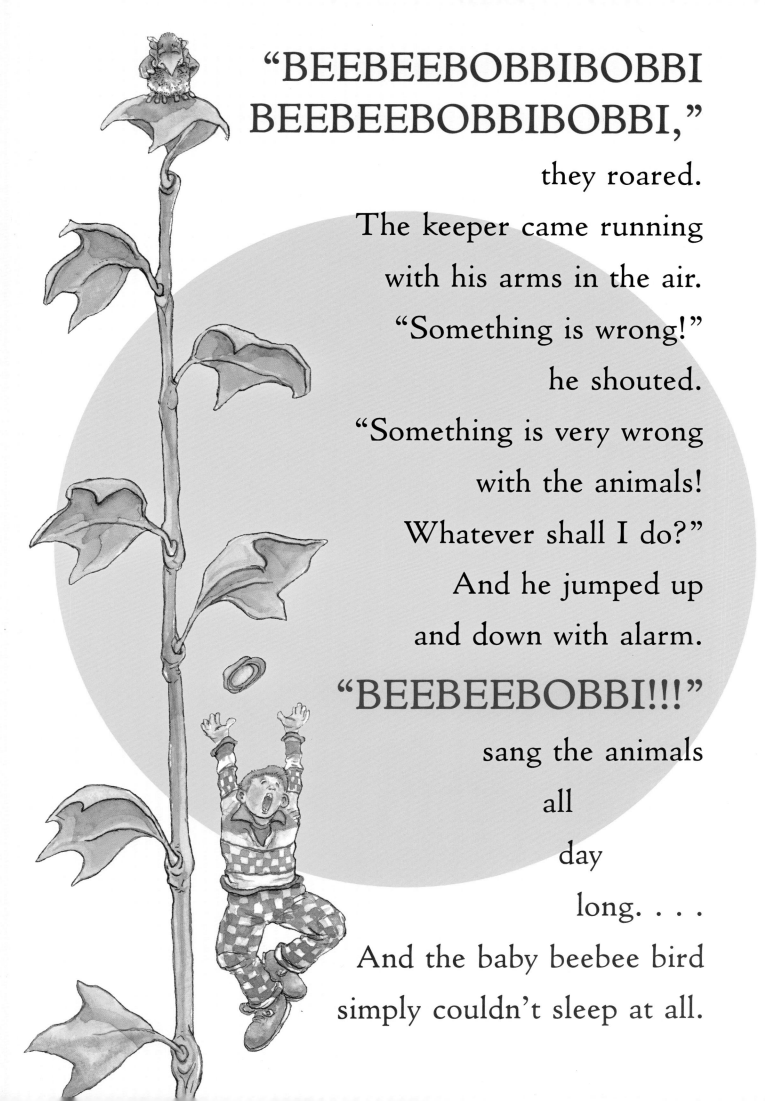

"BEEBEEBOBBIBOBBI
BEEBEEBOBBIBOBBI,"
they roared.
The keeper came running
with his arms in the air.
"Something is wrong!"
he shouted.
"Something is very wrong
with the animals!
Whatever shall I do?"
And he jumped up
and down with alarm.
"BEEBEEBOBBI!!!"
sang the animals
all
day
long. . . .
And the baby beebee bird
simply couldn't sleep at all.

BEEBEEBOBBI BEEBEEBOBBI
BEEBEEBOBBI BEEBEEBOBBI
BEEBEEBOBBI BEEBEEBOBBI
BEEBEEBOBBI BEEBEEBOBBI
BEEBEEBOBBI BEEBEEBOBBI
BEEBEEBOBBI BEEBEEBOBBI
BEEBEEBOBBI BEEBEEBOBBI
BEEBEEBOBBI BEEBEEBOBBI
BEEBEEBOBBI BEEBEEBOBBI
BEEBEEBOBBI BEEBEEBOBBI
BEEBEEBOBBI BEEBEEBOBBI

The sun went down and the moon came up.

BEEBEEBOBBI BEEBEEBOBBI
BEEBEEBOBBI BEEBEEBOBBI
BEEBEEBOBBI BEEBEEBOBBI
BEEBEEBOBBI BEEBEEBOBBI
BEEBEEBOBBI BEEBEEBOBBI
BEEBEEBOBBI BEEBEEBOBBI
BEEBEEBOBBI BEEBEEBOBBI
BEEBEEBOBBI BEEBEEBOBBI
BEEBEEBOBBI BEEBEEBOBBI
BEEBEEBOBBI BEEBEEBOBBI
BEEBEEBOBBI BEEBEEBOBBI

"BEEBEEBOBBI,"
whispered the lion,
who was too tired to roar.

"BOBBIBEEBEE,"
sighed the bear
as he closed his eyes.

"BEE . . . BEE . . . BOB . . . BI . . . ,"
mumbled the elephant,
half to himself.

And then . . . all was still.

The moon shone down upon a sleeping zoo.

Not an ear or a tail or a whisker moved.

And high, high up in the linden tree a tiny bird,
inside a leaf, was fast asleep.

woof
WOWf
woooof

arga
arga
arga
arga

beebeebobbibobbi beebeebobbibobbi beebeeobobb

And now every day at the zoo you can hear
"beebeebobbibobbi beebeebobbibobbi"
in between the lion's roars.

beebeebobbibobbi beebeebobbibobbi beebeeb

ROAR

ROAR

R

ROAR

hiss

But at night there is never a sound.
Nighttime is really best for sleeping . . .
especially for very little birds.